PUFFIN BOOKS

What Stella Saw

What Stella Saw

Written and illustrated by
Wendy Smith

dirty fingernails

lines where fingers fold

life-line

chewed thumb

tide mark line

PUFFIN BOOKS

PUFFIN BOOKS

Published by the Penguin Group
Penguin Books Ltd, 27 Wrights Lane, London W8 5TZ, England
Penguin Books USA Inc., 375 Hudson Street, New York, New York 10014, USA
Penguin Books Australia Ltd, Ringwood, Victoria, Australia
Penguin Books Canada Ltd, 10 Alcorn Avenue, Toronto, Ontario, Canada M4V 3B2
Penguin Books (NZ) Ltd, 182–190 Wairau Road, Auckland 10, New Zealand

Penguin Books Ltd, Registered Offices: Harmondsworth, Middlesex, England

First published by Hamish Hamilton 1993
Published in Puffin Books 1995
3 5 7 9 10 8 6 4 2

Text and illustrations copyright © Wendy Smith, 1993
All rights reserved

The moral right of the author/illustrator has been asserted

Made and printed in Belgium by Proost

Except in the United States of America, this book is sold subject to the condition that it shall not,
by way of trade or otherwise, be lent, re-sold, hired out, or otherwise circulated without the
publisher's prior consent in any other form of binding or cover other than that in which it is
published and without a similar condition including this condition being imposed on the
subsequent purchaser

Stella's mum was a fortune-teller. She worked in a curly-topped kiosk at the end of the pier. During business hours she was known as Madame Z.

She wasn't very clever at telling people's fortunes, but she was so kind she made her customers feel happy. All day long, they queued to see her.

After work she became plain Mrs Fortune. Even so, she spent every evening practising her craft. Stella always had to be on hand.

Stella thought knowing what was going to happen all the time must be really boring. Perhaps it was just as well that despite her many hours of practice Mrs Fortune was not very good at her job.

But this was a big disappointment to Mr Fortune. He was a weather forecaster and always angling for tips.

"Will it be foul or fair today, Madame?" he would ask, trying not to sound too serious.

As for Stella, she had no interest in the weather. She wasn't interested in fortune-telling either. She was mad about football. But her mother could never predict any football results. She didn't have a clue what would happen, not even to Stella's favourite team, Bolden Rovers. And so, Stella saw little point in looking into the future.

Then, one morning as she drank her tea, Stella noticed something odd in the tea-leaves. She looked more closely and

THIS IS WHAT SHE SAW:

"I see a storm in a teacup," she declared.

But Mr Fortune wasn't listening. He was
trying to work out which way the wind was
blowing.

Mrs Fortune took no notice either. She
was on another planet altogether.

"Did you want beans for breakfast,
dear?" she asked her daughter.

"You should know," yawned Stella.

"What I do know," said her mother looking at her star chart, "is that a tall, dark stranger is coming this way."

Mr Fortune's ears pricked up. He feared the stranger might be the Head Forecaster coming to give him the sack. His reports had been going badly wrong recently.

"Will it be foul or fair today?" he asked desperately.

But his wife had gone to buff up her crystal ball.

"Dad! Dad! *I* can tell you," said Stella peering into her cup. "It will be hot and sunny everywhere, but a freak storm will hit Bolden's Cove at 11.47 this morning. A slow-moving anti-cyclone . . ."

Her father blinked in astonishment.

"A storm," he said excitedly. "I must get to work."

As soon as he reached the office he announced the approaching storm. No one really believed him but his boss alerted the coastguard just in case.

Sure enough, the storm hit Bolden's Cove at 11.47 exactly. Thanks to Mr Fortune's warning no boats had put out to sea. His boss was pleased. Mr Fortune was relieved. Stella was amazed.

So was Mrs Fortune when a *small*, dark stranger came, bearing a telegram.

"UNCLE DIGGORY IS DODDERY.
GAMMY LEG. COME AT ONCE.
YOURS, DR CHANCE."

"Oh Stella, your Great Uncle Diggory
has a bad leg. He must be almost on his
knees," she sighed.

"What rotten luck," said Stella sadly.
She was fond of her Great Uncle Diggory, a
keen football fan like her.

So Mrs Fortune shut up shop and went to nurse Uncle Diggory.

While she was away, Stella decided to
have a go at palm-reading. Ever since her
success with the tea-leaves she had been
wondering if there wasn't something to be
said for fortune-telling after all. Wouldn't it
be wonderful to find out who was going to
win the Football Cup Final? But first she
thought it best to have some practice.

She began with her dog Lucky's paw.
THIS IS WHAT SHE SAW:

"You're in for a surprise," she advised
him.

Then she read the girl next-door's palm.

"Wow!" she said. "You will make a long
journey and meet a new friend."

THIS IS WHAT SHE SAW:

FIRST SCHOOLGIRL IN SPACE
MEETS MAN IN THE MOON.

Lastly, she tried to work out the week's weather but she ran out of palms. She used the star charts instead. The next morning her father was thrilled.

"It never rains but it pours," he joked, handing Stella some tea.

Draining her cup she was very excited to see:

THE SCHOOL DAY:

MORNING:
No games:
water on pitch

No French:
teacher on leave

DINNER:

No bouncy
bits in
sausages

No lumps
in gravy

or custard

AFTERNOON:

Boiler
blows
up

Headmaster
blows up

Everyone
sent home
early

Well, the day turned out just as the tea-leaves foretold.

Stella, feeling hopeful, ran all the way home from school. She had been so lucky with her fortune-telling, surely now she would be able to find out whether her team would win the Football Cup Final.

She tried the tea-leaves but she could not read them.

She tried the star charts and the cards but that did not work.

Finally, she dared to try her mother's crystal ball.

At first it was dim and murky. Gradually the picture cleared and Stella was horrified . . .

TO SEE:

"Oh, no!" cried Stella, catching her breath.

That was her club, Bolden Rovers. A huge tree was lying across the pitch. Some players were shouting.

Supposing what she saw were to happen
during the Cup Final? The match would be
ruined. Worse still, someone could be hurt.

She rang the football club at once to
warn them.

"That tree by the goal," she gasped, "it's
going to fall down and . . ."

"Not to worry, lass," interrupted Mr
Sneed, the manager, to sounds of crashing
branches. "The lads are pulling it down
right now. It's been rotten for years.
They're having great fun. Can you hear
them?"

WHAT STELLA DIDN'T SEE:

"Thank heavens!" said Stella, putting down the phone.

She had seen the future all right but not on the day she expected.

She made some tea to calm her nerves. She drank it down and . . .

"Mum!" cried Stella, covering up the crystal ball.

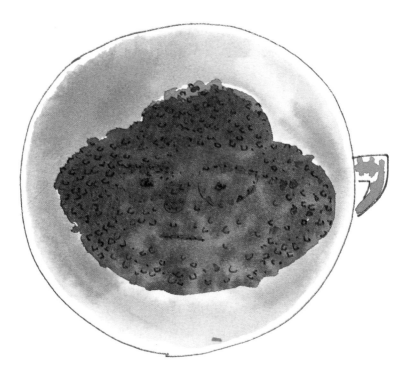

"Best not fiddle with Fortune, dear," said her mother, "unless like me, you have the gift. Now, you'll be glad to hear Great Uncle Diggory is fit and well. Do be an angel, and make some tea."

But Stella gave up drinking tea there and then. She had had enough of the future.

Mrs Fortune carried on her good work at the pier.

Mr Fortune, his confidence restored, became famed for the accuracy of his weather forecasts.

"The weather will be fine and sunny," he declared, "for Saturday's Cup Final."
And it was.

Also available in First Young Puffin

DUMPLING
Dick King-Smith

Dumpling wishes she could be long and sausage-shaped like other dachshunds. When a witch's cat grants her wish Dumpling becomes the longest dog ever.

SOS FOR RITA
Hilda Offen

Rita is the youngest in her family and her older brothers and sister give her the most boring things to do. What they don't know is that Rita has another identity: she is also the fabulous Rita the Rescuer!

THE INCREDIBLE SHRINKING HIPPO
Stephanie Baudet

Simon finds a magic hippopotamus in the garden. It shrinks if anyone says a word meaning "small" and grows again if the word "hippopotamus" is said. Simon loves his new pet, but finds out that it isn't the easiest kind of animal to keep . . .